This edition published by Parragon in 2011
Parragon
Queen Street House
4 Queen Street
Bath BA1 1HE, UK

ISBN 978-1-4075-9946-5
Printed in China

Disney
Peter Pan

PaRragon

Bath · New York · Singapore · Hong Kong · Cologne · Delhi
Melbourne · Amsterdam · Johannesburg · Auckland · Shenzhen

There once was a house in London where a family named Darling lived. There were Mr. and Mrs. Darling and their three children, Wendy, John, and Michael.

Watching over the children was Nana, the nursemaid, who also happened to be a dog. It was to this home that Peter Pan came one magical night.

He chose this house for one very special reason: there were people there who believed in him. But not Mr. Darling—he only thought about business, the importance of being on time and dressing properly.

But Mrs. Darling was still young enough at heart to believe that Peter Pan was the spirit of youth.

8

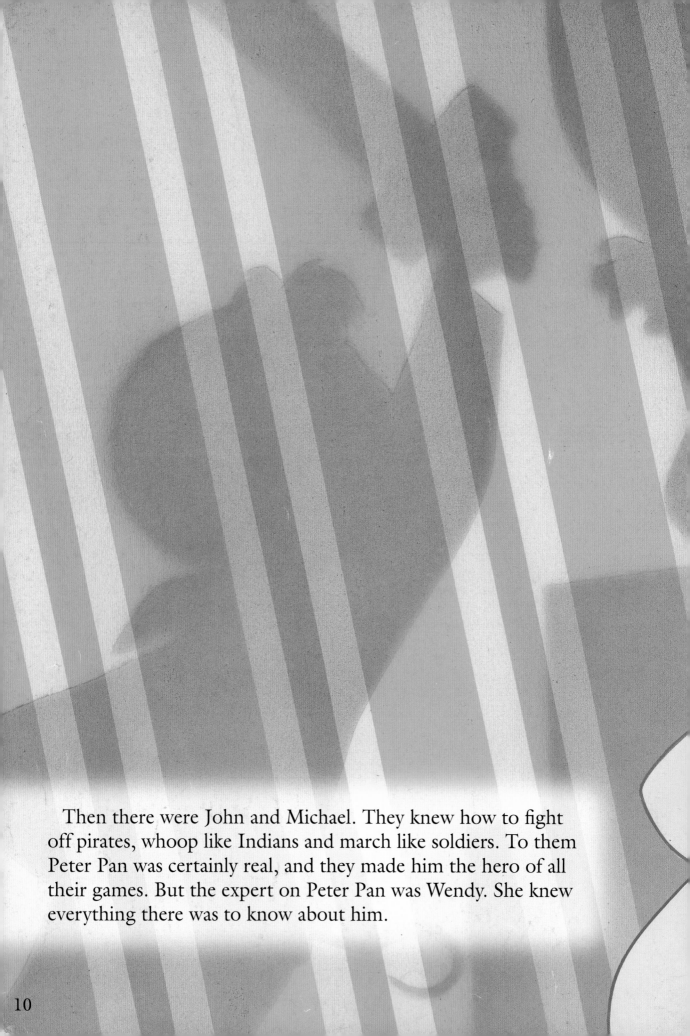

Then there were John and Michael. They knew how to fight off pirates, whoop like Indians and march like soldiers. To them Peter Pan was certainly real, and they made him the hero of all their games. But the expert on Peter Pan was Wendy. She knew everything there was to know about him.

On this particular night, after Michael and John had drawn a pirate map on their father's shirt front, Mr. Darling angrily declared, "The children need to grow up."

Then, turning to Wendy, he added, "This is your last night in the nursery, young lady. And there will be no more dogs for nursemaids in this house."

Mr. Darling promptly marched Nana outside, where he tied her up for the night.

That's how it came to be that when Mr. and Mrs. Darling went out to a party later that night, Wendy, Michael, and John were left all alone, asleep in their room.

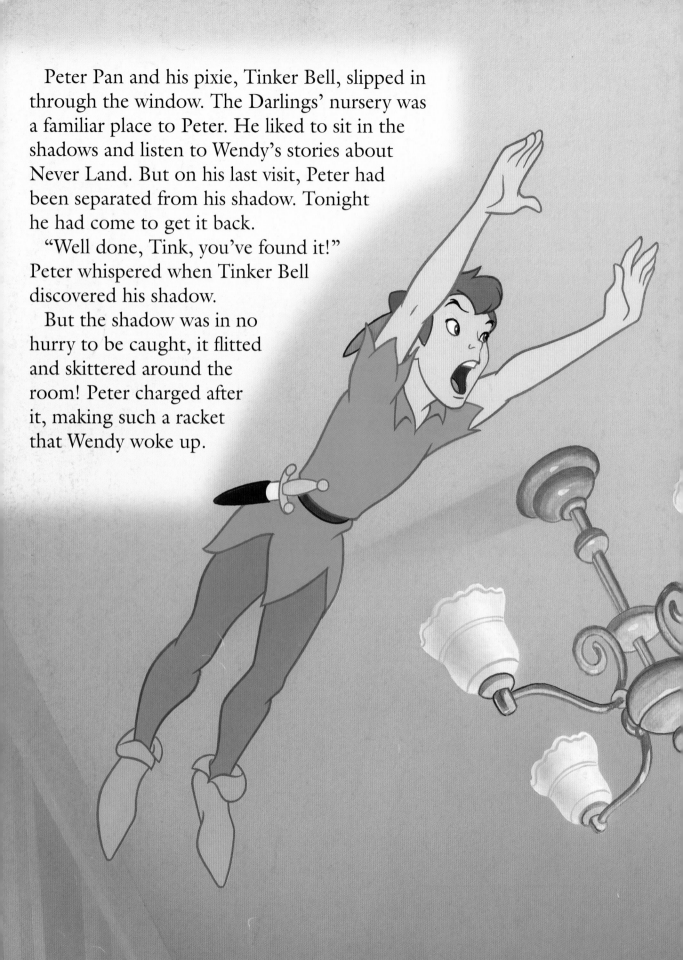

Peter Pan and his pixie, Tinker Bell, slipped in through the window. The Darlings' nursery was a familiar place to Peter. He liked to sit in the shadows and listen to Wendy's stories about Never Land. But on his last visit, Peter had been separated from his shadow. Tonight he had come to get it back.

"Well done, Tink, you've found it!" Peter whispered when Tinker Bell discovered his shadow.

But the shadow was in no hurry to be caught, it flitted and skittered around the room! Peter charged after it, making such a racket that Wendy woke up.

Sure enough, Hook was holding Tiger Lily prisoner and had tied her to a rock in the sea. Peter set off to rescue her before the tide came in.

"I'll show the old codfish. Stay here, Wendy, and watch the fun!" Peter called.

"I've got you this time, Pan!" Hook cried as he forced Peter near the edge of a cliff. Peter backed away but Hook followed him. "Aaaahhhh!" Hook yelled as he tumbled off the cliff! "I'll get you for this, Pan!"

As he fell toward the water, Hook heard a familiar sound... tick-tock, tick-tock, tick-tock. The crocodile was waiting.

"I say, Hook," grinned Peter Pan, "do you hear something?"

The crocodile swallowed the captain! But the terrified Hook fought furiously and jumped right back out!

"Smee! Smee!" Hook screamed as he tumbled into the boat. "Row for the ship! Row for the ship!"

While Smee rowed as fast as he could, Peter swooped down to save Tiger Lily and fly her back home.

The Indian Chief was so happy to see his daughter again that he freed John, Michael, and the Lost Boys. Then he placed a headdress of beautiful feathers on Peter Pan, proclaiming Peter Pan "Chief Little Flying Eagle."

"Waaawhoop!" yelled Peter.

"Oh, how wonderful!" said Wendy.

"Bravo!" added John.

"Peter Pan! I knew you'd come!" Wendy cried. "I saved your shadow for you. Let me sew it on for you. Oh, Peter, I'm so glad you came back tonight, because it's my last night in the nursery," she added sadly.

"But that means no more stories!" cried Peter. "I won't have it! Come on! We're going to Never Land. You'll never grow up there!"

"John! Michael! Wake up...Peter's taking us to Never Land!" cried Wendy. "But Peter, how do we get there?"

"Fly, of course. It's easy. All you have to do is think a wonderful thought. And—" said Peter, shaking Tinker Bell, "add a little bit of pixie dust."

"We can fly!" shouted Wendy, John, and Michael as they followed Peter and Tink out of the nursery window. They soared over the rooftops of London.

Peter laughed with glee as he pointed up into the sky. "There it is, Wendy—Never Land...second star to the right and straight on till morning."

From high up in the sky, they finally spotted the land of their dreams.

"Look, John," cried Wendy, "Mermaid Lagoon!"

"And the Indian Camp!" yelled John.

"There's the pirate ship and its crew," added Michael. "It's just as you told us, Wendy!"

The captain of the pirate ship was Hook. He hated Peter Pan.

"Blast that Peter Pan!" said Hook as he studied a map of Never Land. "If I could only find his hideout, I'd trap him."

Captain Hook got his name because he had a hook where his hand should have been. And who was to blame for that? Why, Peter Pan, of course.

Hook had another enemy, too—the crocodile.

"He's been following me around for years, licking his chops," said Hook.

"And he'd have had you by now, Cap'n, if he hadn't swallowed that alarm clock. Now when he's about, he warns you with his tick-tock, tick-tock..." said Smee.

"Peter Pan, ahoy!" cried the lookout.

Instantly Captain Hook forgot about the crocodile. "Swoggle me eyes," he cried, looking through his telescope. "It is Pan!" He ordered his men to load the cannon and fire!

"Quick, Tink!" shouted Peter as the cannon balls flew by. "Take Wendy and the boys to the island! I'll stay here and cause a diversion!"

Tinker Bell took off at once for Peter's hideout. But she purposely flew too fast, leaving the others far behind.

"Tinker Bell! Wait for us! We can't keep up with you!" yelled Wendy and the boys.

But Tink didn't want to wait. Peter Pan had hardly looked at Tinker Bell since Wendy had come along. Tink didn't like it one bit, and now she had a plan!

Tinker Bell zoomed ahead, flying into an opening in a tree where the Lost Boys and Peter lived.

She told the boys Peter had sent her with a message that there was a terrible 'Wendy-bird' headed their way. Peter's orders were to shoot it down!

The Lost Boys hurried out from their hiding place.

"I see it!" yelled Skunk as he and the others placed stones in their slingshots.

"Ready... aim...fire!" shouted the boys. Suddenly rocks were flying everywhere, hitting Wendy and sending her tumbling from the sky!

Luckily, Peter Pan arrived just in time to catch Wendy.

"Peter...you saved my life," said Wendy, throwing her arms around him.

"I bring you a mother to tell you stories," Peter angrily told the Lost Boys, "and you shoot her down!"

"B-b-but Tink said it was a bird," stammered Cubby.

"She said you said to shoot it," added Rabbit.

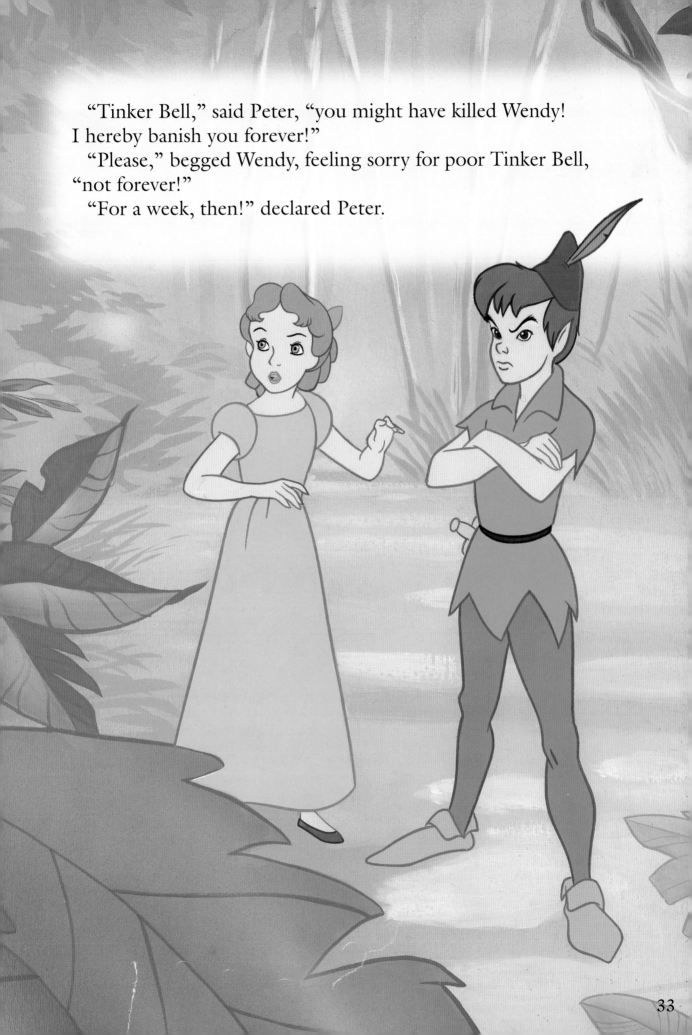

"Tinker Bell," said Peter, "you might have killed Wendy! I hereby banish you forever!"

"Please," begged Wendy, feeling sorry for poor Tinker Bell, "not forever!"

"For a week, then!" declared Peter.

Taking Wendy by the hand, Peter flew off to show her
Mermaid Lagoon. John and Michael wanted to explore Never
Land, too, but had no interest in mermaids. They wanted to
see Indians.

"John, you be the leader," declared the Lost Boys. Then,
lining up behind him, they marched off into the forest.

As they marched along, the Lost Boys and John made a plan.
They would be very clever and capture the Indians!

It might have worked, too, except for one thing—the Indians caught them first.

Michael and John were very frightened until the Lost Boys explained how things worked. "When we win, we turn them loose. When they win, they turn us loose."

But this time the Indian Chief wouldn't set the Lost Boys free. He thought that they had kidnapped his daughter, Tiger Lily.

"You tell me where you hid Princess Tiger Lily," the chief said, "or you'll be punished!"

Meanwhile, as Peter was showing Wendy the lagoon he suddenly spotted Hook and Smee rowing by in a small boat. Tied up in the back was Tiger Lily! "It looks like they're headed for Skull Rock," Peter said. "Let's see what they're up to."

But there was someone who was not joining in the celebration. Poor Tinker Bell was all alone without Peter or her friends, the Lost Boys. And she wasn't happy at all.

And that's just how Smee found Tinker Bell...all alone, sitting by herself.

"Beggin' your pardon, Miss Bell," said Smee, catching Tinker Bell in his cap, "but Cap'n Hook would like a word with you if you don't mind."

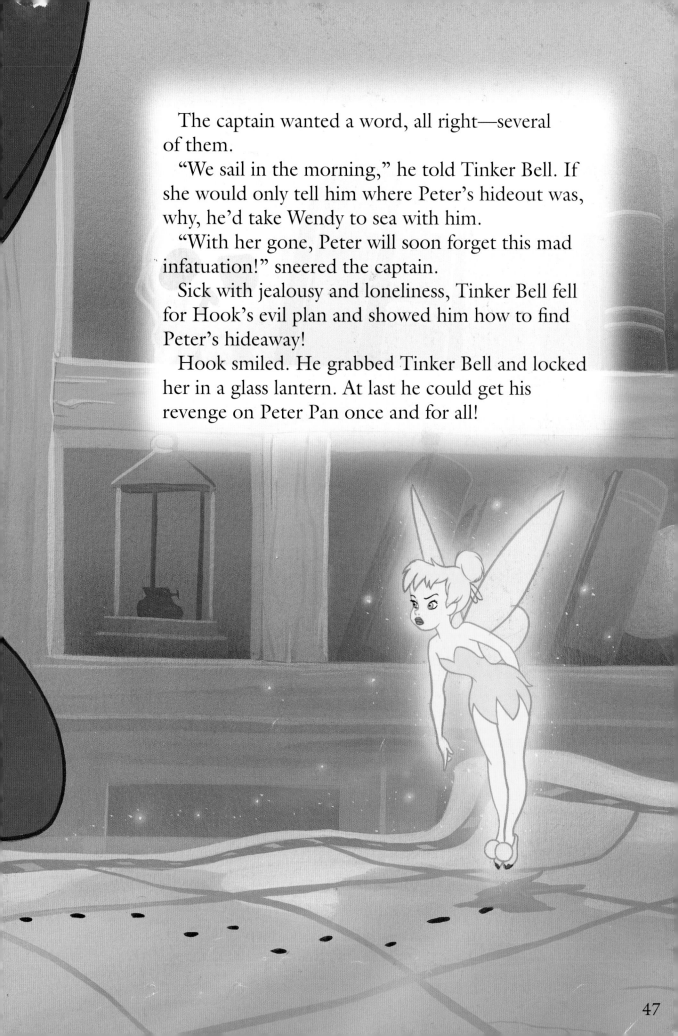

The captain wanted a word, all right—several of them.

"We sail in the morning," he told Tinker Bell. If she would only tell him where Peter's hideout was, why, he'd take Wendy to sea with him.

"With her gone, Peter will soon forget this mad infatuation!" sneered the captain.

Sick with jealousy and loneliness, Tinker Bell fell for Hook's evil plan and showed him how to find Peter's hideaway!

Hook smiled. He grabbed Tinker Bell and locked her in a glass lantern. At last he could get his revenge on Peter Pan once and for all!

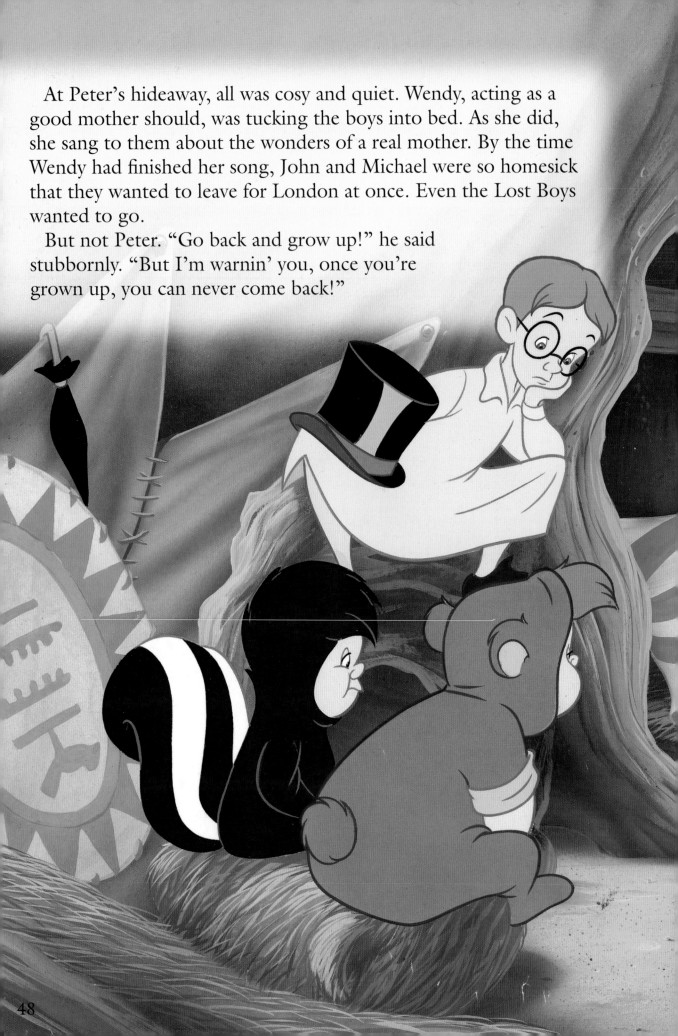

At Peter's hideaway, all was cosy and quiet. Wendy, acting as a good mother should, was tucking the boys into bed. As she did, she sang to them about the wonders of a real mother. By the time Wendy had finished her song, John and Michael were so homesick that they wanted to leave for London at once. Even the Lost Boys wanted to go.

But not Peter. "Go back and grow up!" he said stubbornly. "But I'm warnin' you, once you're grown up, you can never come back!"

But no one was listening to Peter. They had only one thought on their minds: a mother to love them and hold them and sing them to sleep at night.

One by one, the boys left Peter's hideaway—only to walk right into the arms of the waiting pirates!

"Now to take care of Master Peter Pan!" chuckled Hook as he lowered a beautifully wrapped package into the hideout.

Tying his prisoners to the mast of his pirate ship, Hook warned them, "Join us or walk the plank."

"Never," declared Wendy. "Peter Pan will save us."

"My dear," said Hook, "we left a present for Peter, a sort of surprise package. I can see our little friend at this very moment, reading the tender note, 'To Peter, with love, from Wendy.' Could he but see within the package, he would find an ingenious little device set so that when it is six o'clock he will be blasted out of Never Land forever!"

Hearing Hook's evil plan, a desperate Tinker Bell knocked over the lantern where Hook held her prisoner. Crack! went the glass. Tinker Bell was free!

Off she flew to try to save Peter.

Back in his hideout, Peter Pan picked up the package and was just untying the bow when Tinker Bell flew in.

"Hi, Tink," said Peter, holding up the box. "Look what Wendy left for me."

Tinker Bell tried to pull the package away. "Stop that!" yelled Peter. "What's the matter with you?"

There was no time to explain. Tink flew at the box, pushing it as far from Peter as she could. The gift began to smoke. And then... KABOOM!

The explosion was so huge, it rocked the pirate ship! Hook removed his hat and bowed.

"And so passeth a worthy opponent!"

Smiling, Hook turned to the captive children. "Which will it be? Join my crew or walk the plank!"

Wendy spoke up bravely. "Captain Hook, we will never, ever join your crew."

Hook gave Wendy his most gentlemanly bow. "Ladies first, my dear!" With tears trickling down her cheeks, Wendy walked along the plank.

One step, then another, closer and closer to the edge, until finally...she jumped!

"Cap'n," said Smee, "there was no splash!"

"The ship's bewitched!" the men began to wail.

But it wasn't a ghost who had come to haunt Hook. It was Peter Pan, along with Tinker Bell! He had come to save Wendy!

"This time you've gone too far!" shouted Peter Pan as he flew up onto the rigging.

Hook scrambled up after him, then drew his sword.

"Take that!" cried Hook as he lunged at Peter, forcing him off balance. "I'll run you through!"

Peter quickly flew out of Hook's way, cutting this way and that with his dagger.

"You wouldn't dare fight old Hook man to man," taunted the captain. "You'd fly away like a cowardly sparrow."

"I'll fight you man to man with one hand behind my back!" crowed Peter.

As Wendy, John, Michael, and the Lost Boys fought the pirate crew, Hook took a powerful swing at Peter. But the captain lost his balance!

Down, down, down fell Captain Hook...to face his worst fear. The crocodile was waiting, and its mouth was wide open!

The last Peter, Wendy, John, Michael, or the Lost Boys heard of the terrible Captain Hook were his calls for help. "Hooray for Captain Pan!" screamed all the children.

"All right, ya swabs," said Peter Pan to his brand-new crew, "we're castin' off!"

"But...but...Peter," stammered Wendy, "could you tell me, sir, where we're sailing to?"

"We are going to London, madam!" said Peter.

"Michael, John, we're going home!" Wendy smiled.

"Hoist the anchor!" cried Peter to his crew. "Tink, let's have some pixie dust!"

Tinker Bell flew all around the ship, sprinkling her magical dust as she went. Then up, up, up, went the ship, and as it rose, it began to glow like gold.

"Wendy," said Mrs. Darling. She was gently shaking her daughter, whom she had found asleep by the window.

"Oh, Mother, we're back!" announced Wendy as she woke.

"Back?" asked Mr. Darling.

"All except the Lost Boys," explained Wendy. "They weren't quite ready to grow up. It was such a wonderful adventure! Tinker Bell and mermaids and Peter Pan. We sailed away in a ship in the sky... "

"Mary," said Mr. Darling, not sharing Wendy's excitement at all, "I'm going to bed."

But as he turned to leave, Mr. Darling paused to look up into the night sky.

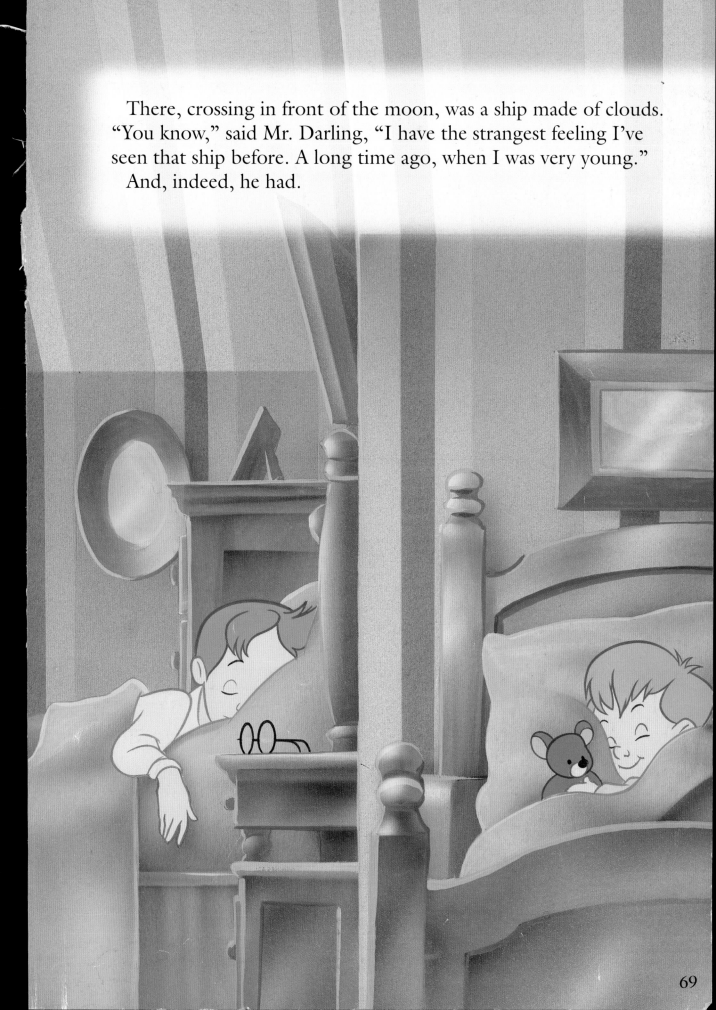

There, crossing in front of the moon, was a ship made of clouds. "You know," said Mr. Darling, "I have the strangest feeling I've seen that ship before. A long time ago, when I was very young."

And, indeed, he had.